JILL HEINERTH

THE AQUANAUT

ILLUSTRATED BY JAIME KIM

tundra

When I was young, the world
seemed too dangerous.

Everything was too hard.
Places were too far away.
I was too young.

My parents kept saying,
"Maybe when you are older . . ."

But that was okay because I had
a big imagination.

When I was young, I wanted to float
through space and see the moon up close.
It shined so bright that I didn't mind
soaring into the darkness to get there.

I wanted to help others.
It made me feel grown-up.

I wanted to know what it was like
to be something else. Could I grow
flippers or a beautiful tusk? Could I
talk to a dolphin?

I wanted to fly. (Who doesn't?
Superpowers are cool!)

I wanted to explore new worlds and meet new friends.
I wondered what my new friends might look like.

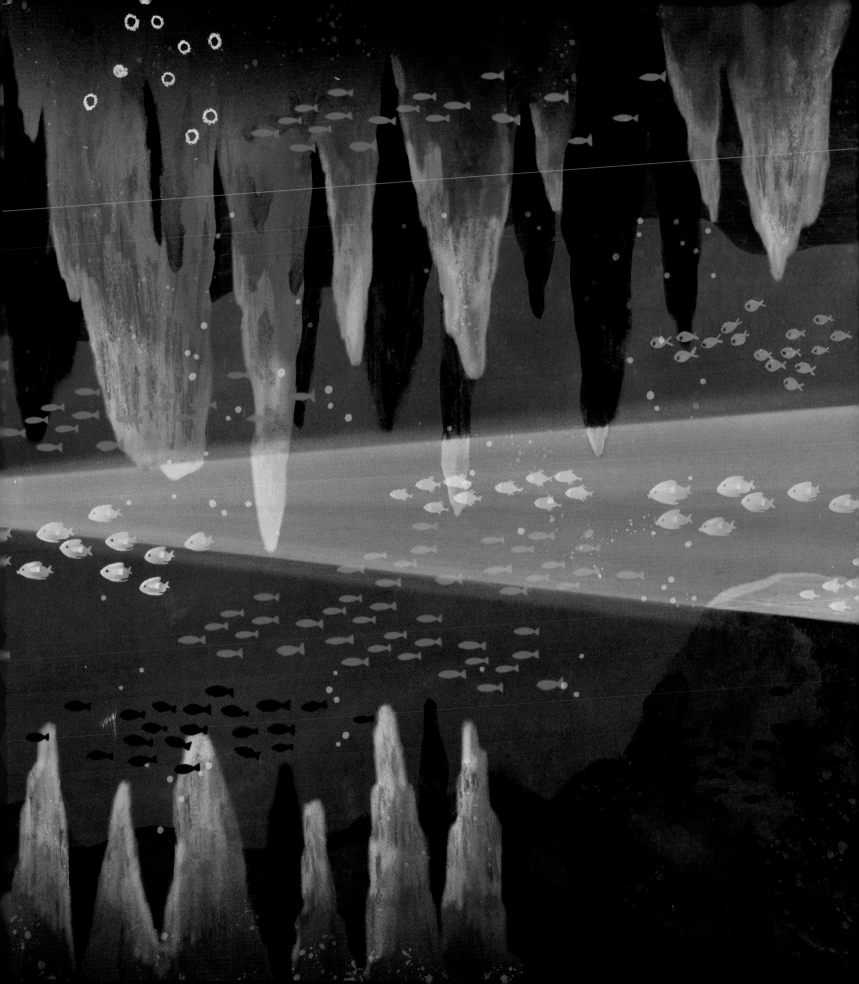

I wanted to be brave. (I was scared of the creatures hiding in the dark.)

I wanted to travel into the future to see what I would become. I knew anything was possible.

AUTHOR'S NOTE

When I was young, I wanted to be an astronaut. But instead of going to outer space, I decided to explore dark, cavernous spaces on Earth. More people have walked on the moon than have been to some of the remote places I have discovered right here on our water planet!

Today, I am a cave diving aquanaut and an underwater photographer. Using some of the same gear that astronauts wear, I swim through water-filled caves beneath your feet in fantastic new worlds that nobody has seen before. When I was young, I decided to make my dreams come true. My big imagination helped me to become an explorer. Where will your big imagination lead you?

Swimming with moon jellyfish (no stingers!)

PHOTO: JILL HEINERTH

Floating through underwater caves

PHOTO: JILL HEINERTH

Filming inside an iron mine

PHOTO: CAS DOBBIN

Taking a selfie with sea lion friends

PHOTO: TRISHA STOVEL

To everyone who feels different: you are remarkable. — J.H.

For Jaeho — J.K.

TEXT COPYRIGHT © 2021 BY JILL HEINERTH
ILLUSTRATIONS COPYRIGHT © 2021 BY JAIME KIM

Tundra Books, an imprint of Penguin Random House Canada Young Readers,
a division of Penguin Random House of Canada Limited

LIBRARY AND ARCHIVES CANADA CATALOGUING IN PUBLICATION

Title: The aquanaut / Jill Heinerth ; [illustrations by] Jaime Kim.
Names: Heinerth, Jill, author. | Kim, Jaime, illustrator.
Identifiers: Canadiana (print) 20200153420 | Canadiana (ebook) 20200153471
ISBN 9780735263635 (hardcover) | ISBN 9780735263642 (EPUB)
Subjects: LCSH: Heinerth, Jill. | LCSH: Scuba divers—Biography—Juvenile literature.
Classification: LCC GV838 .H45 2021 | DDC j797.2/34092—dc23

Published simultaneously in the United States of America by Tundra Books of Northern
New York, an imprint of Penguin Random House Canada Young Readers,
a division of Penguin Random House of Canada Limited

LIBRARY OF CONGRESS CONTROL NUMBER: 2019956929

Edited by Elizabeth Kribs
Designed by John Martz
The artwork in this book was created using watercolor and digital techniques.
The text was set in Eames Century Modern.

PRINTED AND BOUND IN CHINA

www.penguinrandomhouse.ca

1   2   3   4   5   25   24   23   22   21

tundra | Penguin
Random House
TUNDRA BOOKS